Arthur T Woodward

Songs from a Studio

Arthur T Woodward

Songs from a Studio

ISBN/EAN: 9783744768825

Printed in Europe, USA, Canada, Australia, Japan

Cover: Foto ©Andreas Hilbeck / pixelio.de

More available books at **www.hansebooks.com**

SONGS
FROM A STUDIO

BY
ARTHUR T. WOODWARD

MELBOURNE: GEORGE ROBERTSON & CO
MDCCCXCIX

TO

THE BROTHERHOOD OF SONG.

Melbourne, April 6th, 1899.

CONTENTS.

Preface : p. xiii.

SONGS FROM A STUDIO:

ix.

SONGS FROM A STUDIO:

SONGS FROM A STUDIO:

xi.

PREFACE.

DURING every hour I have spent in an attempt to produce a work of Art, I have breathed the breath of life and inhaled happiness. I have always found Peace and Companionship in some nook of Nature's Garden, or in a corner of my Studio, with either a brush or a book in my hand.

The commendation or condemnation of one's work can only exhilarate or exhaust, as the case may be, for a brief period of time ; while Art's friendship is Eternal, and an immortal possession.

The attempts here made have been to render artistically, moods which may, or may not, once have been mine. Should they prove cheering or helpful to any one during their march along the clogged and stony pathway of life, then I shall be glad that I yielded to persuasion and allowed them to be published.

ARTHUR T. WOODWARD.

Melbourne, April 6th, 1899.

A VOLUNTARY.

WORDS are but fragments of unuttered thought,
    Songs are but words kissing each others lips,
    Music love's footsteps as along she trips ;
  Love is life's balm, from Heaven to each one
      brought,
Life, but a breath, so soon by Death upcaught,
  And back across the Night to God it slips.

LET'S PLAY WITH TIME
(Rondel.)

LET'S play with Time, for Time with us doth play,
    Make him our slave and chain him by our side!
    Lash him if he refuses to obey,
    And check his wild career through space so wide.

He's but a shell of emptiness, of pride
    And bustling arrogance, we hate—so say,
    Let's play with Time, for Time with us doth play,
Make him our slave and chain him by our side!

Let's clip his mighty wings this very day
    And leave him groaning, and his wrath deride,
And heed him not, and dance and laugh away,
    Turn night to day and age to youth beside!
Let's play with Time, for Time with us doth play,
    Make him our slave and chain him by our side!

3.

THE LAND OF THE NIGHTINGALE AND ROSE.

THERE is a land idyllic, glad and gay,
   Where love and song alone are ever rife,
   Where aught else is a trifle, and where strife
  Is quickly charmed by melody away ;
There magic music plays by night and day,
 And fingers deft bewitch the lyre and fife,
 In sylvan bowers of love all pass their life
Midst halcyon years of hope and holiday.
O let me dream and never wake again,
  And live with troubadours and wed the rose,
And hear the nightingale in her refrain
  Trill of delight, of undisturbed repose
For painter-poet's heart and glowing brain,
  Where he may muse and canticles compose.

ON LOOKING AT MY MOTHER'S PORTRAIT.

I CANNOT speak, much less attempt to sing,
    I cannot play, for lute in twain is riven,
    Nor clearly see, for tears fast forth are driven
    And flood mine eyes, and little solace bring ;
The picture of thy sainted self doth sting,
    And make acute my loss, which long I've striven
    To think were gain, for often in a sweven,
Thy seraph voice I heard through Heaven ring.
I knew thee only in my infant years,
    And cannot of myself remember thee,
Yet thou hast ever quelled my brooding fears,
And grief, at loss of what to me appears
    Man's greatest trial here ; and made me see
God's wondrous wisdom through my surging t ears.

5

EXULTATION.

THE swallow's come over the sea
 And brought a sweet message for me ;
 And the lark lilts anew on the wing,
 For his voice through the welkin doth ring,
And proclaims me as joyous as he,
 That I live, that I play, that I sing,
 Nor my lot would exchange with a king.

The dawn wears a buoyant light tread
With footprints all rosy and red,
 And the sky has the light for its mate
 And the day is no longer sedate,
For the night has forever now fled,
 And the sun never sets till it's late,
 And the world is all love and no hate.

6.

The breeze sings a song as it plays
And kisses the sun's dancing rays,
　　While the trees stretch their limbs to the skies
　　And with happiness grow and uprise ;
And the monk always chants, never prays,
　　For he feels what I know now and prize
　　As he views the old world with new eyes.

Fair Clytie a lover hath won
And tells of the joy now begun ;
　　And the butterfly flits to the flower
　　And requests it to make her a bower,
For to-day she was kissed by the sun,
　　By Apollo, who gave as a dower
　　All his glory, his love and his power.

The birds trill a new spring-like note
With a frenzied and fluttering throat,
　　And the insects and things of the earth
　　Now delight in new love and new mirth,
And harmonies round me now float,
　　For at last love has given life worth,
　　And the world now enjoys a new birth.

The waves do not wail as they flow
And storm-clouds in sky never show,
    For the ocean and air are a-tune
    And the sun is now wed to the moon,
And Love will force sorrow to go,
    And smother her while in a swoon,
    For she dreams of entranced honeymoon.

No longer there's parting of ways
All hearts and all voices give praise,
    For Death has at last lost its sting
    And all cares and all woes take to wing,
And love crowns us with laurels and bays,
    Lo, the sea and the earth to us sing,
    And the love-bells in Heaven now ring !

A CRUSADER.

TRY as I will, I cannot keep a-tune,
　　Or strike the strings with trembling, tender
　　　　touch.
　I am December, rarely flaming June ;
I cannot walk without a stick or crutch—
A singing mendicant, and known as such—
A dying ember, burnt and spent too soon—
A shadowed sun, a chilly, sickly moon—
　A battered atom never meant for much.
And yet a whisper-waft will to me say,
　" Cheer up, old soldier, in thy great crusade
Against hypocrisy, for from the fray
　Thou shalt emerge a hero.　Be thou staid ;
　Ne'er heed thy shattered frame.　Lo, thou hast paid
For thy despair, so sing and play away !"

LOVE'S BLOSSOM.

I AM no bard with lyre or lute well worn,
    To sing about love's blossom brought through
           space,
    Held in Night's hand and guarded till the dawn
Of Life, by God, till it took up the place
Allotted it, in this its earthly race.
I am no seer or sage to tell why born
To live in ease or poverty forlorn ;
    Enough to sing that by an act of grace
Divine, this little fragment of delight—
    Of Him, who born of Mary, mother mild,
    Long ages past,—is sent, an angel-child.
Nothing more lovely, balm to weary sight,
Than babe pressed to its mother's breast so tight
    On which its God and parents all have smiled.

THE MIND.

O PINNACLE and summit of the man,
　　We bow to thee and know thy unseen power
　As keystone of life's arch, so wide of span
　　And dizzy loftiness! Our fortress, tower
　　Of strength, and guide in every doubting hour.
I cannot find thee in thy hiding place,
　Nor have I wish to drag thee into light ;
　Thou art too sensitive for searching sight,
　　Too complex in thy parts for hand to mend,
　　Too mystical for man to work and tend,
And kept agoing only by God's grace.
　　Be ever thou our solace, comfort, friend,
And always wear a smiling, helpful face,
　And be a lighted lamp when dark is night.

CHIAROSCURO.

BRIGHT joyous bird in yonder tree,
Trilling such gladness, mirth and glee,
Thy blitheness, hateful mockery
To one whose soul is as a note—
A sound—which, without mate, doth float
Musicless, sad, in skies remote,
Banked up with threatening cumuli,
Whirled about space, and never free
To harmonise in melody.

The sunshine—which thy plumage gay
Reflects in colours, makes thy day
One long warm happy holiday—
Ne'er reaches me.   Those sunlit trees
Throw shadows cold, filter warm breeze
To chilly blast, and my blood freeze.

Thy lustrous lights meet sun ere yet
It gilds and fringes veins of jet,
And droop asleep when it hath set.
Mine eyes, so dim with bitter tears,
No sun can see.   Through long dark years
Not one warm ray thawed frozen fears.
My throat gives forth no song at all,
My head ne'er rests at calm nightfall ;
Light verdant earth seems funeral pall.

Oh ! I with you would gladly change,
And as soon used to wings now strange
Would fly away to mountain range
Or highest Alp, to dizzy height
Far above clouds, obscured from sight,
Nearer to God, nearer to right.
There from that giddy peak I'd scan
The heavens above, that mystic plan
Divine, and see just what is man
And what he's for, why sin is rife—
Why not a bird with nestling wife
Wooing and warbling all his life.

TO A CANARY.

YOU daffodil dream of delight,
      Refreshing to ear and to sight,
      With your song and your plumage so bright.
      Never fear
For I'm near,
And I hear
Your sweet accents in symphonic flight.

You cannot soar up to the sky
And poise in the air as you fly,
And your wings you can never now try.
What a shame !
For your fame
I'll proclaim,
And the seraphs above will draw nigh.

14

It's jealousy, envy and greed
Prevent you from flitting o'er mead.
So you're caged by a monster, indeed!
Sing a verse?
No, a curse;
Or, what's worse,
For his soul let the Devil now plead.

I'd love to throw open the gate
Which debars you from living in state
As the Prince of the birds, with a mate;
And I'll try,
By-and-by
To bring nigh
A Princess for a sweet *tête-à-tête*.

You essence of music and life,
You must take to yourself a wee wife
To cheer away gloom and all strife,
And, when blest,
Build a nest
And have rest,
Let no heartache prevail and be rife.

15

You'll woo her and love her as well,
And stories of chivalry tell,
And in dreams you will live in a dell,
Nothing rue,
Love and woo,
Trill anew
While your feather-friends ring marriage-bell.

O brave little light-hearted joy,
You chirruping, painted live toy,
With your life so mixed up with alloy,
Heave no sigh,
Neither cry
Nor be shy,
For your music and mirth I enjoy.

For ever I'll be your true friend,
And always to you will attend,
While you live and your messages send
Of true love
From above,
Yellow dove,
For your spirit with mine seems to blend.

EVENTIDE.

THE sun is lingering ere it says Good-Night,
The sky is drawing curtains o'er the day,
The Moon is rising with her regal sway,
And soon will reign in majesty and might ;
Forms become formless in Eve's dusky light,
Color is sombre and the world seems gray,
Man trudges wearily his homeward way,
Dales lose their depth and highest hills their height.
Oh, let me linger, too, and let me dream,
And let me take my poet-book and lyre,
And let me be just what I am, not seem,
And I will sing of her, my heart's desire,
Of love, which is to me the thing supreme,
Of smiles and kisses and of passion's fire.

SUCCESS.

WHAT does it matter if the tune's all wrong,
 Or if the notes collide when at their play,
 If there's no meaning in my joyful lay,
 If incoherence in unruly tongue ?
Obstreperous joy, like eagle wild and strong,
 Controls my muse and wayward lute to-day,
 Now strikes a fugue, now sings a roundelay,
And will not keep atune for very long.
Oh, heed me not, or listen to the din
 Of jumbled sounds and twangings of the lyre.
It is but roysterous mirth, not ugly sin,
 That's born of ecstasy, and will not tire ;
  For there has come what long I strove to win—
Success, the pinnacle of Life's desire.

IRISES.

GAY-WINGED goddesses of rainbow hues,
   You bring to life my dormant fitful muse ;
      Could you but cut the thread which chains my
        soul
    To this live corpse, and then my death-knell toll

Your love for me would prove that legend, which
Some folk conceive was hatched in brain of witch :
   What care I what they think, if only thou
   Couldst by such act wipe anguish from my brow.

Sweet serving-maids to Juno's majesty
In mythic days of nuptial revelry,
   Diffusing color at that civic *fête*,
   Tinting the throne on which they proudly sate.

But stay ! These aberrations of the mind
Not only reason, but my eyes, do blind.
   For lo ! you're lovely feathery flakes of snow,
   Spring blooms, not goddesses of long ago.

No oceanides ye, no sea-nymphs bare,
But queens of hill and dale and landscape fair ;
　　Your thrones, young tufted grass, from which you rise
　　Shielded by swords, pointed to sapphire skies.

You once supplied the clouds with water, when
Jupiter deluged earth ; and now again
　　Appear in multi-colored flowers sublime,
　　Goddesses still of color and springtime.

O'er all the earth you reign, and still impart
Rapture and gladness to each aching heart ;
　　From pondering o'er thy beauty I now cease,
　　For to my wearied soul you've brought sweet peace.

LOVE'S LAMENTATION.

IT cannot be,
    That God intended all my years to be from
        thee ;
                        It cannot be.

It cannot be,
    No matter how I yearn to love and cherish thee ;
                        It cannot be.
It cannot be,
    Though I would fling my heaven-born aim to earth
      for thee ;
                        It cannot be.

It cannot be,
    Though brightest day is blackest night if not
      with thee ;
                        It cannot be.

It cannot be,
    Though veilèd night thy beauty cannot hide
      from me ;
                        It cannot be.

It cannot be,
  Though dazzling suns could never blind my eyes
    for thee ;
                                    It cannot be.

It cannot be,
  Yet o'er this bare, bleak world I'd wildly search
    for thee ;
                                    It cannot be.

It cannot be,
  Though I would prove by facing death my love
    for thee ;
                                    It cannot be.

It cannot be,
  No matter that in every dream I live with thee ;
                                    It cannot be.

It cannot be,
  Though master-passion strong as death con-
    sumeth me ;
                                    It cannot be.

22

It cannot be,
      Though red-hot brand thy image cannot
        sear from me;
                           It cannot be.

It cannot be,
      E'en though I'd steep my soul in sin to fondle
        thee;
                           It cannot be.

It cannot be,
      Though I in deepest Hell would gladly live
        with thee;
                           It cannot be.

It cannot be,
      E'en though in those sad eyes a look there is
        for me ;
                           It cannot be.

It cannot be,
      Till by the tomb my spirit is at last set free ;
                           It cannot be.

WHY?

WHY throbs my soul? Why beats my pulse so strong?
Why is my lyre lit up with lambent flame?
Why does my voice keep singing one sweet
name,
And will not change the tune or change the song?
To me the melody seems right, not wrong;
I play it by the hour with loud acclaim;
Lips never cease, but love it just the same,
And sing the dulcet sound with tireless tongue.
It is the name of all the names 'neath Heaven,
The sweetest note in highest seraph's voice,
The key which keeps my harpsichord a-tune,
The word most sung by my persistent steven,
The song alone which makes my heart rejoice,
The inner brightness of love's harvest moon.

TOO LATE.

ONWARD some struggle, though the Night is nigh,
And find their Death; yet love they never knew—
While others love too well, too deep, too true,
And only feel an unresponsive sigh,
And walk alone through all Eternity.
And some there are—and they are not a few—
Whom if their lives they could commence anew
Would trill all day, like lark athwart the sky.
For by a hard and seeming cruel Fate
They met their love, but could not then embrace ;
Alas ! Alas ! Ah, yes ! They met too late !
Too late ! Too late ! In its divided state
One soul, one spirit, Destiny did face,
And said, Adieu ! hopeless and desolate.

SOMEDAY.

BOLD " Expectation," mailèd cap-à-pie,
    Walks by the side of his *faire ladye* kind,
      Fighting all foes who come not from behind—
    A marching corps of doubt. He cannot see
All round; and hidden " Someday " treacherously
    Puts shaft in bow, ready to shoot through wind
    An arrow which this armoured knight may blind,
Who fights for love to all eternity.
So through the dark dense wood he beats a track
    For her to walk upon, and hopes the way
    Will not be long and drear, so not to stay
A night in tangled, mazy scrub, and ne'er, alack,
    Get out and reach the moated grange they may
    Enjoy and dwell and die in peace, Someday.

LIFE'S MIRROR.

IF time would only stop and sun stand still
  For one short span,
 We should have time to add up life's long bill,
  Which few now can.

Our past might seem a rugged, rambling road,
  Which oft was dark,
With no one to relieve us of our load,
  Which left its mark

On some by scarrèd wounds and furrows deep
  And streaks of grey—
Still ever eager shrouded fate to meet,
  Be what it may.

Those days of childhood's innocence and mirth
  Life's dawn would seem—
Winged, and on tip-toe scanning dusky earth,
  Now waning beam.

27

Our days at school, when dux or dunce we were,
    Were days indeed;
All, men and women were—we then could bear
    What now we heed.

To some those schooldays would recall much joy—
    Their happy days—
Life one long holiday without alloy,
    Spent in much praise

Of varied games and brutal childish sport,
    Of fights and feeds,
And acts designed by devils' brains they thought
    Delightful deeds.

Others, those days would fill with ripe regret—
    Acutest pain;
The chances lost their lives ne'er cease to fret
    And darkly stain.

Long hours of work and use of midnight oil
    Some would recall;
A feebled frame, through years of mental toil,
    Is now their all.

Bright stars of talent never had to " stew
       Like others had ;
Schooldays to geniuses are ne'er too few—
       Revive naught sad.

Those sandbuilt structures, castles in the air,
       Built and rebuilt,
Are crumbled into dust, have left nowhere
       One sweat-drop spilt

On sullen soil, in which life's seed's oft sown,
       And springeth forth
A weakly weed, which soon by Fate is mown
       In fitful wroth.

Our early loves, would like a meteor flash
       At night, appear ;
Life's magic mirror, now seen bright, would crash,
       Then disappear.

We would untie for visionary glance
       Life's roll of schemes,
Mildewed and marred.   Recovering from the trance
       (Saddest of dreams)

Might pause and ponder plans we drew
        And dwelt upon,
And only now should see them riddled through
        With imperfection.

Our adolescent years, with all they brought
        And did unfold,
We'd own at once they many a lesson taught,
        Yet never told

Or e'er disclosed those secrets and desires
        Long closeted.
The youthful lighting of those early fires
        Now nearly dead

Made us delight in life, in fancied bliss ;
        No star foretold
That ills and death to some would follow this,
        And wreck the mould

In which their budding life had been designed
        And damned at birth ;
They did rejoice, left pleasures not behind
        (Of such no dearth).

No spectre haunted their mad revelry
    With merry kin ;
'Youth must be youth,' so let desire be free
    And feast on sin !

Such items of our life are in its bill—
    And costly too ;
They never can be paid, erased, until
    We pass from view.

To some those days of growth brought years of life,
    Of love and peace ;
Their righteous deeds save them from fret and strife
    Till life's release.

Life's mirror is to them supremely bright,
    Reflecting all
Things good and beautiful ; their evening light
    Makes gay Death's pall.

Our ups and downs would there be surely found
    In varied inks.
Successes gained by fraud are scored all round,
    Great faulty links

In life's long chain of lies, deception—base
        As bastard brass,
In which we rarely righteous purpose trace,
        Alas ! Alas !

Those few who have their conscience kept alive,
        Unstained and pure,
Will from their bill of life great joy derive,
        And pay it sure.

Our days of courtship, love and great content,
        Of reckless vow,
Illumine what is dark ; bright flashes sent
        To blind us now.

Some would here find a line in deepest red—
        And not too red,
Of their unholy love ; naught need be said
        How it was fed.

While others here would read 'tween maddening lines
        Of their disgrace,
Would see here mirrored, long past frightful fines,
        And vice embrace.

No trifling number—would shut close their eyes
                And turn their face
To lusts recorded plain ; man's smile they prize—
                Scum of their race !

And worse than that, not fit on earth to dwell,
                And Hell too good
For all such loathsome brutes, corrupt as well,
                And if one could

Such wretches should be thrown to ravenous beasts
                And torn to shreds,
Their rotten bodies making putrid feasts.
                Their swollen heads

Could serve as playthings for those birds of prey
                Which hover near
Wherever carrion is, then fly away
                Knowing no fear.

And some would see those maidens mild, whom they
                Thought they did love,
Who, after marriage bells, found that, to stay,
                Peace from above

33

Came not to their sad home—each loved their best,
    Which love was hate.
Real, rapturous love, they neither one possessed,
    Such was their fate.

In glancing back, some too would dimly see
    Lost hearts, all torn
And bleeding still, swimming in agony,
    And much love-worn

Through years of tender trusting, love and care
    Of one, who knows
The love can ne'er be shared—ill-mated pair—
    Their past we'll close.

And some would see in history's silvered glass
    Love's young long dream,
Filling two lives with joy, which quietly pass—
    A blithe sunbeam.

A few would find on pages torn and rent,
    Black deeds and crime
For which they've paid, and now are penitent,
    Effaced in time.

Others would note marked lines of praise for deeds
  Both great and grand
In arts and war, in commerce or in creeds—
  A noble band.

Our loved ones passed to rest we'd picture now,
  Nor wish them here ;
They know true bliss, they know the victor's brow.
  We shed a tear

Which slowly dims and blears their image seen
  In ancient frame ;
We hardly dare believe that they have been,
  Like us, the same

Weak, weary, worn-out travellers on this road
  So long and rough,
On which so many miles we've borne our load,
  And long enough.

Ah, well ! it's best that rushing time ne'er stops
  Or heeds our call ;
Death, scythe in hand, us one by one still lops,
  And down we fall.

Far better let me look ahead and there
        That future see,
Of rest and peace and love, where life's despair
        Won't trouble me.

Far better stare in covered future's face
        Till my eyes tire ;
Maybe she'll lift her veil, and there might trace
        My heart's desire.

A SUPPLIANT.

OH, let me kneel and linger at thy feet
   And humbly worship as a priest at prayer!
   Oh, may thy eyes in mercy my eyes meet,
   And may thy heart my pleadings feel and greet,
And may thy face approving aspect wear,
No finger indicate my quick retreat,
But beckon me to share thy smile and seat,
   And save me from the pangs of love's despair!
Let me, like gallant knight, thee homage pay
   And live and die for thee and be thy slave,
Appointed minstrel, and by night and day
Sings songs of love, and thrilling music play.
   Oh, bid me come, as ocean bids the wave!
Do bless and pity! Turn me not away!

PEACE.

HIDDEN Elixir for embittered life !
    Art thou on earth, in air, or ocean deep ?
    Dost thou,if gained,free all from troubled sleep,
    And from the world remove its grief and strife
And soothe sad brow, like hand of loving wife,
  And, like her, troubles calm and near us keep ?
  Wilt thou, when found, level life's hill so steep,
And scalp our foes with fierce unerring knife ?
Answer at once ! we long have pondered well
  Over this problem most persistently ;
If so, we ready are to search in Hell,
  In Heaven, and earth and sky or surging sea,
  If thou but say man can discover thee
And live in peace, too sweet for song to tell.

MADRIGAL.

O LILY-WHITE rapture! O hazel-eyed flower!
  The sunniest beam of life's sunniest hour;
    O piece of perfection, from forehead to feet!
    Say, how should a lover approach thee and greet?

O wonder of wonders!　O queen of the light!
Fair fusion of brilliance, of joy and delight!
  Bright star of the starlight! O centre of space!
  Bewitching and charming from tip-toe to face!

Thou scatterest fragrance in brake and in bower;
An exquisite perfume enriches each hour
  Of the day and the night when thou walkest abroad,
  And the fairies now dwell where thou lay on the sward.

No lover were worthy of gaining thy hand,
Yet not even saint could thy beauty withstand;
  Oh, say, for thy love may I hope and have part?
  May cheek lie by cheek, may heart beat against heart?

HUMILITY.

O BARD Supreme, Divine, exalted, great,
Conductor of High Heaven's immortal band,
Before Whom angels and arch-angels stand;
Teach us humility, for mind's estate
So often proud becomes, and too elate
With knowledge and its fame athwart the land;
A greater judgment and Hell's fire well fanned
Doth learning—if it heeds not Thee—await.
Oh, give us grace, great Master-poet, Friend!
And steep our souls in sounds produced above,
And let the Future with the Present blend.
Oh, may our life and scholarship but tend
To make us live for God and seek His love,
To serve Him solely and His song extend!

THE GOLD-DIGGER'S TENT.

FOUR girls in a tent, and grand girls too,
    With eyes of black, brown, grey and blue,
    They fill the digger's bushland home
    With jovial laugh 'neath canvas dome,
Which rings through the scented atmosphere, ·
Brings to his eye a timid tear,
Carries him back to a distant year,
Recalls the voice of a lost one dear,
More precious than all the gold yet won,
For they lived in holy unison.
These giddy girls little dream that he,
A roughish shell on life's rough sea,
Possesses a heart which never was sold,
A brighter hope than burnished gold.

They're out for the day, as you will guess,
Wandering about bush wilderness.
The clouds grew black, the rain came on,
They flew to his tent, right glad he'd gone
To his hole in vale of sand and waste,
And little cared for that bitter taste
Which is always in his soul so dry
From shedding salt tears and agony.
They knew that his tent in shady glen
Would shelter them till it cleared again.
They think of themselves, are heedless, gay,
And leave the digger to dig away,
To dig till he drops with spade in hand,
Till his soul has reached " The Golden Land "—
For all they care. Oh ! why shouldn't they
Enjoy all they can ? Why should they stay
Till the digger's return to waste a word
Of cheer or thanks to one of a herd
Of dirty, rough, common digging brutes,
Who delve in the earth midst stones and roots
Like a worm—but forget that even they
May in spirit blend with God, and pray
And send up thanks for mercies sent
From Him to this earthly firmament.

THE LITTLE MESSENGER.

TWO little feet for months have passed this way ;
  Two little hands each noon have laden been ;
  Two little eyes have often smiled " Good day ;"
  Two rosy cheeks from week to week I've seen.

Two little feet now seldom pass the bay
  At which I sit and pen a line of song ;
Two little hands are empty every day,
  And cheeks are pale and often mute her tongue.

No daddie's sweetheart takes his can of tea
  And packages of things for him to eat :
His shift is done.   A fall of earth, and he
  Sailed in Death's boat Eternity to meet.

43

A LOVE LYRIC.

OH, SING me a song of love,
 Of love and but love alone,
And sing of that fair fond dove
 In melody's sweetest tone.

And tell me that I am blest
 With love that is life and soul,
And strike the strings with a zest
 That oceans of love may roll.

Oh, sing me the song to-night,
 For my heart is all a-tune ;
' Oh, sing it in daffodil light
 In a nook, and sing it soon.

Oh, sing it and let me die
 As the last sound fades away,
And bury me by-and-by,
 But love me for aye and aye.

FLOWERS.

HAS this earth a delight like a flower,
   With its beauty, its fragrance and power?
   Could there be such a mingling of charms—
   For our rapture and peace it embalms,
And our happiness seems to enjoy,
And never our senses doth cloy,
   And sings us sweet sonnets and psalms?

Is there one in this world such a friend
As its ear to our hearts it doth lend,
   Who will listen with face quite demure
   To the plaint of the lover—not sure
That the maid of his heart and his eye
Will consent to be his by-and-by
   As a flower—than which none can be truer?

Is there aught in this world so attired,
Or by everyone so much admired,
   With its features so perfect of line,
   And its colour and contour divine,
And its bearing so stately and sweet,
Or so rare and so rapturous a treat
   As a flower—which is yours and is mine?

Is there anything makes us exclaim,
Or suggests or inspires us the same
　　With such gladness and mirth and delight,.
　　Or a dirge if our day is Death's night—
Is there aught else of which we ne'er tire
And long for and love and admire
　　As the flower of the field and our sight ?

Earth's jewels are surely its flowers,
Which adorn and make lovely her bowers ;
　　They are gems of rare brilliance and fire
　　Which her maids for her garments desire—
For she always is seen quite a-blaze
And makes love to the Sun in spring days,
　　To his kingdom and crown doth aspire.

They are singer and minstrel in one,
And the hearts of the nations have won ;
　　They give bliss to the breeze as it sighs,
　　And throw joy to the bird as it flies,
And glamour to eve's fading hour,
And to verdure its passion and power,
　　And the love in our life which we prize.

At marriage times flowers are then seen
More regal than monarch or queen,
   And are modest and nothing disdain,
   Yet are gorgeous, and gloriously reign,
And are gracious to humble and great,
Loving all, and no one do they hate :
   God's perfection, without flaw or stain.

He gave them to Earth as her dower
To remind her of Him and His power,
   To delight and to ravish her eyes,
   To solace and soothe when she sighs,
And to be her attendants by day,
And at dusk perfumed music to play,
   And to light up the tomb when she dies.

White flowers are her tenderest shroud
When Death with her mysteries crowd
   Round her soul as it flits to the Light
   From which it once strayed in the night,
And for which it has ever since sought
With the fervour of saint sore distraught,
   And the flowers then illumine its flight.

They were there at the birth of the world
And smiled to the storm as it swirled,
    And welcomed the Day and the Night
    When shivering and shuddering with fright,
And then scented the newly-made air,
And bowed to the lion and bear,
    And completed Creation's grand sight.

HEART'S DESIRE.

HOW happy could I be, with thee through tombs o
time,
How gladly would I live with thee in heat or ice-
bound clime ;
No king would be as proud, or with him would I change,
Or yield one pressure of thy hand for realms of vastest
range.

How sunny were my days, with thee to give them light,
How friendly were the darkness which is now a fearsome
night,
How eager were the clouds to disperse and flit away,
How promptly would my gladness grief's December
turn to May.

How buoyant were my steps, which now are tired and
worn,
How comforting life's vesture, which is now so rent and
torn,
How easy would be work, which now is hard to do,
How smiling would be nature's face, now hidden from
my view.

49

How happy, oh, how happy! yea, happy could I be!
So let me feel the rapture of a touch and smile from thee;
    Oh, let me share that nook where a year seems but an
        hour,
    Where the birds and daisies tell of thy beauty and
        thy power!

How much I need thy pity, for Hope is life to me;
Oh, break the bonds that keep my heart from bounding
        up to thee!
    Oh, send me words of love by a minion of the Moon,
    And let spirit mix with spirit, and two hearts play
        single tune!

TO SLEEP.

WELCOME, sweet siren! Hither come and stay
    And sing a nocturnelle, seductive maid,
    And charm me while my draft of sleep is
      weighed.
Thou art day's azure vest just turned away
To other worlds, leaving your lining gray
    To fold the drug by heavenly chemist made,
    Which as diffused causes mind's flower to fade
And close in sleep, who is betrothed to day.
Oh, let me woo this pale-faced sainted nun
    And throw aside her trailing dusky dress
    Which hides her form and mars her loveliness!
    Oh, let me upward gaze into those eyes
    Downcast so long, and which are all I prize,
Her lips impearl with kisses, holy one!

A DREAM.

ONE night I dreamed I stood at Heaven's gate
    With thee, O loved one, for my sainted bride :
    Lo! Peter and his angels said, " Too late !
    Ye cannot pass ; ye cannot wed inside."
Then sinking on the steps disconsolate
    We wept in anguish, for on earth we tried
    To be together, but we were denied,
And now we were refused that hallowed state.
Our wails and lamentations brought in haste
    A messenger from God 'neath golden dome,
    Bringing our passport for that Brighter Home
Towards which we'd travelled o'er life's barren waste ;
    And great and stormy was His righteous wrath—
    He struck the earth with flame, lashed sea to froth.

ALONE.

WHAT is home without its children ?
What is life without a mate ?
Only Dead Sea fruit and ashes,
Only brine and bitter fate.

It is sky without its glory,
It is sun without its glare,
It is breeze without its freshness,
It is gloom beyond compare.

It is lute without its player,
It is bird without its note,
It is eye without its moisture,
It's a ship that will not float.

It's a world without its sunshine,
It's a sea without its shore,
It's a boat without a rudder,
It's a heart without a core.

It's like love without a lover,
   It's like king without a state,
It's like tree that will not blossom,
   It's like fiend without his hate.

It is night without its moonlight,
   It is fire without its flare,
It is earth without its verdure,
   It's a trap without a snare.

It is song without its gladness,
   It is gold without its worth,
It is grief without its wailing,
   It is laughter without mirth.

It's like God without His mercy,
   It's like Satan without sin,
It's like Hell without its fury,
   It's like war without its din.

Such is home without its children,
   Such is life when spent alone,
When no wife is there to comfort,
   When no love or kiss is known.

When no hand is ever ready
    To give aching brow its peace,
When no children's merry prattle
    Has in slumber found release.

It is day without its sunrise,
    It is night with twilight rare,
It is dusk without its love-light,
    It is dawn with blindest stare.

Such is home with loveless firelight,
    Such is room with single chair,
Such is house on chilly evening,
    Without firelit face so fair.

When no rippling, nestling tresses
    Deck with gold the pillow slip,
When no snow-white arm caresses,
    When no kiss joins lip to lip.

It's like Earth without its Heaven,
    It's like Heaven without its Earth,
It's like moon without its minions—
    Without mate of priceless worth.

TO A BUSH-BIRD.

YOU blithesome, singing bird with voice so clear,
   I wish you'd come and perch quite near
     To me, while here I paint all day,
     Drowning my sadness with your liquid lay.

I've never seen you, but I'm sure you are
Among the birds, as sun to star;
     " Fine feathers make fine birds," they say,
     But plumage bright doth wither and decay.

Not so your song, which from your soul doth rise
In praise to God in Paradise,
     From whom all blessings do descend:
     A broken heart, your song may one day mend.

So sing a chant with your melodious voice,
In which I'll join, and too rejoice;
     For thou hast freed me from all pain,
     Kept Hope alive and brought me love again.

TO FOLLY.

FLIRT away
　　Happy fay,
　　Sing and trill and dance and play—
　　Make your life a holiday
　　Ever and for aye.

Have no fears,
Shed no tears,
For to you life now appears
Like the May-time of the years,
And your wildness cheers.

Love yourself,
Flatter pelf,
Honesty put on the shelf,
Virtue know not flighty elf,
Please your fairy self.

Heed not me,
You are free,
And as pretty as can be,
Skip with Cupid o'er the lea
Like a honey-bee.

Hearts are won
By such fun,
And if by it they're undone,
It is nothing, giddy one,
    You are not a nun.

Night and day
Wield your sway
Over monks and men that pray,
Make them chant a love-sick lay,
And to them you say :

" Holy sires,
Light love's fires
While the incense slow expires,
For my love your heart perspires;
Wooing never tires—

Know you bliss?
Like a kiss?
And, if you it much should miss,
Do not fret and frown and hiss,
    Penance do, like this.

Fast and weep,
Never sleep,
And your soul in sin now steep,
You can't buy my love too cheap
And its rapture reap,

Till you do
Nothing rue,
And uproot the weeds that grew
Out of sham and mockery, too,
And are made anew.

And unless
You confess
That love got you in distress,
I will never you caress
Or you touch and bless.

Then you may
Homage pay
For one minute every day,
But you cannot near me stay
If you preach and pray.

When at last
Anguish's past,
And with me your lot is cast,
I will spurn you, furious, fast,
And your peace soon blast.

Am I fair?
Do I care?
Not two atoms of the air;
I with no one long will pair,
Woo me now who dare!"

TROUBLE.

IT is a lane that's long, that has no turning, dear !
  Be brave of heart
  And play thy part,
For with me at thy side, there's naught to fear, my dear !
  So struggle on again
  Along life's dreary lane.

It is a heart that's dead, that ceases beating, dear !
  So clasp my hand,
  We can withstand
All storms and enemies as they appear, my dear !
  So, to me cling, and we
  Shall soon its turning see.

THE FIRST-BORN.

SHE'S really a little lump of love,
    A gold-crowned lily from Heaven above;
    Lies in her cot and well within view—
    Very like me and very like you.

Wrapt in the robes of the night she came,
Without identity, needing name,
Filling our hearts with wonder and glee—
Very like you and very like me.

A wee, wee bundle of various charms,
Stout little legs and chubby fat arms,
Ringlets of gold oft kissed by the sun—
Pink personality, like two in one.

Roseate rapture! life with love a-swim,
Grandfather's darling, and much like him,
Deep, dreamy eyes of violety blue—
They say she's like me, and yet like you.

Perfect blush blossom, so fresh and fair,
Daintiest, loveliest, anywhere,
A priceless treasure, for us so new—
Is she like me, or is she like you?

O infinite mystery, vast sublime!
Whose earthly term's but a tick of time,
Now just embarked on life's unknown sea—
God made her like Him, and you and me.

THE VIGILS OF THE NIGHT.

DURING still watches, from sunrest until dawn,
    When night is guest with dusky, trailing train,
    Thoughts chase on thoughts and come and flit
        again
With her, in that grey gown, at chilly morn.

Those anxious watches of the night bring light
    And life to some.   A first-born very fair,
    Joy lulled their pain, which vanished in night air ;
Daybreak brought smiles, not tears, to their glad sight.

Those aching, yearning watches for relief,
    Which some will never get, and must live on
    In agony and anguish.   All is gone
From them ; both day and night are drowned in grief.

Those dark, expectant wakings of the night,
    Which end in light and love and marriage ties,
    Bring life's great joy and zest to some pure eyes,
Heartsease and ecstasy and great delight.

Those dreary, drawn-out vigils in some cell
    Of vice or crime, perhaps, repentance bring
    For some; maybe, the dawn their death-bell ring;
Toll for a sin, no dirge of mine may tell.

To some, night watches are as silver sand
    On brightest, gayest sunlit smiling shore;
    Their dawn brings faith in God for evermore,
Their morning clasps His outstretched, helping hand.

Those weeping, wailing hours to some lone heart,
    Bleeding and torn, but bring home in the night
    A reeling, tottering wreck—a sad, sad sight;
Each sound her shattered nerves doth jar and start.

Those moonlit vigils are to some a chance
    For praise and prayer for those upon the sea—
    The fisher-folk whose lives are never free
From danger as their crafts o'er billows dance.

To some, their fretting vigils in the dark
  Recall to memory some long-lost one dear;
  Night after night, day after day, a tear
Glides down their cheek in deepest furrowed mark.

To some, night vigils buoyant are as air,
  Bring spring-like love and hope, and one so dear,
  No gloom nor grief is in their heart, nor fear—
One gem in setting twain, enraptured pair.

Those stern and pallid watches of the night—
  When Death is wrestling hard with Life for one
  Whose spirit may have flown ere dawn of sun
To where there is no night—never bring light.

To some there are no vigils of the night,
  For they have bliss and peace beyond compare,
  Sheltered by Him whose love is holy, rare,
Basking in sunshine and eternal light.

A NOCTURN.

IT was moonlight when I met thee first so many
         years ago,
    And for long I heard the echo of your whispered
        silvery " No."
I remember how we parted on that boulder by the sea,
And the moon had lost her brightness, seeming oh so
        dark to me.

It was moonlight when we met again, in now far
        distant years,
And its joyful light made diamonds of thy streaming
        living tears.
As of yore we sat again upon that boulder by the sea,
Trembling, speechless, and the moon shone, oh so
        brilliantly.

BALLADE OF YULE-TIDE.

CHRISTMAS again is here,
  Carols and anthems ring,
 With charity and cheer
  The air seems all a-sing,
The birds are on the wing,
And from each window-sill
  They canticle and bring
"Peace and on earth goodwill."

Best day of all the year,
  When joy doth sadness fling
Away, and love draws near,
  And life has lost its sting,
  And Hope with practised sling
Doth hatred quickly kill
  And says to everything,
"Peace and on earth goodwill."

The world with Godly fear
        Now hails its new-born King
And wipes away each tear,
        Happy and chorussing,
        Bells peal gay, ding, dong, ding,
Sway and are never still,
        Chiming with gleesome swing,
" Peace and on earth goodwill."

ENVOY.

Priest, all will one day cling,
    Clasp hands o'er dale and hill,
Bound by this golden string,
    " Peace and on earth goodwill."

A SEA SONG.

OF help there's need !
　　Winds and sea hiss, the levin's freed,
　　　　The seas begin
　　　　With fiendish grin
To rage and roar, and then proceed
　　　　To wreck and ruin.

Ruin and roar
Abound about that storm-struck shore
　　　　Wailing with woe.
　　　　Revenge forego
And cease thy lashing evermore,
　　　　And calmly flow !

Flow, flow and play,
And ripple round thy beauteous bay,
　　　　And sing and chime
　　　　To varied time
Symphonies bright and sonnets gay
　　　　And chants sublime.

Sublime and grand,
And past man's ken to understand
          Are thy concerns ;
          He rarely learns,
He's but a spark and must be fanned
          Before he burns.

Burns for a space,
Then flickers out and leaves the race
          That's never done
          And never won,
That always goes at lightning pace
          And long begun.

Begun,—Ah, Yes !
And many, failure must confess,
          And vanity,
          Insanity
And folly, in attempting to possess
          The land and sea.

Sea ! mighty sea !
Rolling on towards eternity ;
          Take for thy theme
          Nature supreme,
Man's insignificance to thee,
          Immortal stream !

Stream of all streams !
Awful thy anger often seems,
  Avenging sea !
  Yet prettily,
With varied charms, thy surface teems,
  Glowing with glee.

Glee and unrest,
Ceaseless and tireless, looking best
  Each new-born day,
  In fresh array ;
O tossing gulf from east to west,
  Sway away, sway !

Sway, saunter, swing,
Thy serving waves forever sing,
  And keep a-tune'
  And smile as June ;
One day thou'lt stop ! thy dead upspring !
  And may be soon.

POCHADE.

WE two together long have walked,
    Of love, of life and death have talked,
        And scanned much mystic lore;
            The tune I set, your heart has played;
    And hands to hands have often strayed,
And now as times before
    My Soul,
O thou whom I adore!
        Dreams crown us one exultant whole,
Ever and evermore.

From visions wake, while life abounds
In melodies and summer sounds,
    And veilèd bliss in store;
        Oh, come and be my peerless bride,
    And cleave and cling about my side,
Happy as heretofore
    My Soul,
Happy as heretofore,
        And linger at the lover's goal,
Ever and evermore.

DEATH.

WHAT means this whispered, spectral word called
    death?
    Why at its mention dost thou stand aghast,
    And at its advent fight it to the last,
And struggle to retain departing breath?
Why brood if in the tomb thou slumbereth,
    Or if existence is no more and past?
    Why fret because Time hurries on so fast,
And Doom thy days, O atom! compasseth?
O troubled voice, shrill sounding in the night,
    Amid the silent sovereignty of space,
And majesty of vastness and of might;
One day thou shalt attain life's hidden height,
    Presumptuous particle with questioning face!
And learn Death's meaning through the Infinite.

AN ECHO.

HOW many times
        Has this same form arisen in the eastern
            states of love,
        A dazzling, golden, gorgeous-plumaged
            all-confiding dove ?
How many times ?
How many times ?

How many times
        Have these proud lips proclaimed eternal love
            and music made,
        And blanched as they sighed "Yes" to wild
            devotions, nobly paid ?
How many times ?
How many times ?

How many times
        Will Fate permit thee in love's garb to dwindle
            to her ghost,
        Then lilt again and love again, O piece of flesh
            at most ?
How many times ?
How many times ?

BALLADE OF REMEMBRANCE.

DISTANCE draws halo round thy hallowed head,
  Absence delights in dreaming of those days
  When lips made music and no word was said ;
  Memory, her gallery of Art displays
And never tires of giving silent praise
To one more beautiful than all the rest,
Whose mystic image, ever to me pressed,
  Wafts me a-wondering to that sovran time
When thou wilt nestle in my bowered nest,
  O centre of my vision and my rhyme !

Fortune is frowning with a brow of lead,
  Fate veils the future with a stifling haze,
And over Hope a pall of snow has spread,
  And chords of sadness mingle with my lays ;
  But still I smite my lute along the ways
And fight all foes, though not in armour drest,
And live in hopes of one day being blest
  By thee, thou fairest flower of any clime,
Of all my aims, the summit and the crest,
  O centre of my vision and my rhyme !

Fantasy sings and has Defiance wed,
  And makes the lagging months enchanted Mays,
She feels no fear, and naught in Night doth dread,
  And has for mates a gleesome troupe of fays
  Who dance and gambol while the bell-bird plays
A rhapsody of love with tireless zest.
Though far away, thou still art first and best,
  Thou maid of maidens, saintly and sublime ;
But lo! the days now reel with vague unrest,
  O centre of my vision and my rhyme !

ENVOY.

Angel ! sweet comrade, thou who fires my breast !
Full perfect woman in thee manifest ;
  Alert I am to catch each echoing chime
That comes afar from thee, my spirit-guest,
  O centre of my vision and my rhyme !

THE FIRST KISS OF LOVE.

A LIQUID pearl,
A dew-drop on a rose,
A sun-kissed golden curl,
A summer doze.

Dawn's dreamy blush
Of rosy-tinted dye,
Mantling with silent rush
Life's pale-grey sky.

A mystic thrill,
A quivering of the soul,
Love's lark-like trembling trill,
Life's longed-for goal.

To parchèd lips
Nectar in golden bowl,
Drunk in sweet eager sips
While love-bells toll.

Hear
On rc
A dre
Raptu

A fre:
Ecsta
Life':
Is lov

HER LETTER.

DEEP down a pocket, threadbare, patched and rent,
There hides a letter which to me was sent
Long years ago—
The date I know,
And when I touch it my lone heart doth glow.

It there has lain—though tattered, dirty, torn—
Inside a match-box, pieced and backed and worn ;
Each lonely day
For her I pray
Who lived with me a year, then passed away.

I read it every morn at break of light,
And every solitary cheerless night ;
I see her too,
Though hid from view,
And this old missive seems for ever new.

These few faint lines of writing to me seem
An echo of the past, a living dream,
      Light up the way
      On which I stray,
Old, feeble, weary, lonesome, grave and gray

Will it, I wonder, last intact and whole
Till I have reached life's now not distant goal?
      The day is late,
      Cruel my fate,
For long I've been alone disconsolate.

When it is time, with me it must abide,
And in the mould be buried at my side,
      Clasped to my breast,
      Welcoming rest,
And with me, till the Dawn, cease our sad quest.

THE CHILD AND THE ROSEBUD.

O LITTLE one, with blossom at thy breast,
Immortal flower, a living, loving rose,
The fairest bud that in the spring-time blows,
A tinted lily, tiny angel-guest,
In radiant innocence and beauty drest,
While rippling sunshine from each feature flows.
O miracle ! Each day my wonder grows,
Thou flowering joy and perfume of the best.
Alas ! the bloom that swoons and clings to thee,
And droops and dwindles graceful to the last,
And decks thy infant bosom daintily,
Is but a symbol of a flower that's cast
From Heaven upon the waves of life's vast sea ;
Its petals pale ; thy blush is ever fast.

THE THREE TRAVELLERS.

OLD reeling, rattling, rotting, rumbling car,
   Giving your patrons many a jerk and jar,
   Wheels loose and swaying on their axles bent,
   Covering and cushions showing many a rent

Old weather-worn and weary, worn-out horse,
   Flogged day by day with whips and language coarse,
Many's the trip on this rough road, so bad,
   Many the smiles, many the scowls you've had.

Old drinking, drivelling, dreaming, driving man,
   Closing your days as fast as ere you can ;
Face, fierce and flushed, eyes bleary, sunken in,
   Serving as mask for soul as black as sin.

Old tottering travellers, tired and torn you are,
   Each better days have seen, which nought did mar,
Bearing your burdens with no soul to save,
   Eyes tightly shut to death and your sad grave.

TO A POET-FRIEND.

SWEET singer of the Brotherhood of Song,
        Who knows the secrets of all hidden things,
        Who hears the music that the zephyr sings,
    And feels the pulse of right as well as wrong;
Thou art the friend of creatures ocean-deep,
    The mate of birds with strong up-soaring wings,
    Apollo's help when shafts of light he flings,
And pard of beasts that in the jungles sleep.
Thou hast a tune for every hour and day,
    A song for North and South and East and West
We hear their melody along life's way,
And feel their helpfulness, and listen till
    We marvel, as they echo thy behest
Across the meadows and from hill to hill.

THE CHANT OF THE SOUL
IN SEARCH OF REST
(Chant Royal)

O WINGED winds and waves with lion roar!
    Dost thou know secrets not for man to know ?
    Art thou the friend of things beyond this shore ?
    Canst thou to us life's unseen mysteries show ?
Long have I battled with a great unrest,
Long have I looked for some much-travelled guest,
    Some sage or seer or wizard of the night,
    Explorer of those spheres far past our sight,
Or saint from Heaven above or fiend from Hell,
    To say where, on some mead or mountain height,
The climber travel-spent may rest and dwell.

O breezes, billows, speak, I now implore !
    Subside, and for one moment cease to blow,
If thou hast aught of good for me in store,
    Or canst point out a part of earth below
Or sky above where weary souls are blest,
And where no fret nor fume their lives infest,
    Where night is never dark, but filled with light,
    Where wrong is missing, and where only right
Abides.   If so, oh to me talk and tell
    Of that sweet spot, where in a region bright
The climber travel-spent may rest and dwell !

O constellations ! Heaven's jewelled floor !
   Ye silent listeners to my joy and woe,
Tell to the birds that kiss thee as they soar
   Where there is Peace, that thither I may go—
Matters it not if North, South, East or West—
For long have I pursued this tiresome quest
   And felt my chance of failure far from slight,
   Producing but despair and no delight.
Oh, cannot ye my fears and doubts dispel,
   And name some land where angels do invite
The climber travel-spent to rest and dwell ?

Shall I peruse old tomes of antique lore,
   And will great guidance from their pages flow ?
If I read long and study more and more,
   Would they on me their confidence bestow ?
Why then I'd read with never-tiring zest,
For, oh ! I long to live where life is best
   And purest, and where nothing doth affright,
   But where the spirits of the dead recite ;
" This is the land where all is truly well,
   And here in vestments of the purest white
The climber travel-spent may rest and dwell."

Must I grope on through Death's dark corridor
   And search through states aflare with angry glow ;
And failing, must I scan God's kingdom o'er
   And analyse the colours of the storm-cloud's bow ?

Must I ask seraphim my zeal to test,
And plead with nature's forces to suggest
    Some ritual, some mass or holy rite,
    As means by which a distraught mortal might
At last discover some sweet soothing dell,
    Where after weary search and ceaseless fight
The climber travel-spent may rest and dwell?

ENVOY.

Giver of life! Great God the Infinite!
Time! Change! Doom! Death and Devils! oh, unite!
    And chanting, show where Love and Truth expel
The palest sin; for there, O soul a-plight,
    The climber travel-spent may rest and dwell.

ERRATA.

Page 4, Line 11, *for* .. " her" .. *read* " his."
 ,, 10, ,, 6, ,,   " or "   ,, " nor."
 ,, 11, ,, 2, ,,   " thy "   ,, " thine."
 ,, 18, ,, 9, ,,   " or "   ,, " nor."
 ,, 19, ,, 7, ,,   " thou "   ,, " you."
 ,, 19, ,, 8, ,, " could'st " ,, " could."
 ,, 19, ,, 8, ,, " wipe anguish from my brow" *read* " recast my life anew."
 ,, 19, ,, 14, ,,   " my "   ,, " mine."
 ,, 20, ,, 11, ,,   " thy " *read* " your."
 ,, 22, ,, 2, ,,   " my "   ,, " mine."
 ,, 23, ,, 2, ,,   " thy "   ,, " thine."
 ,, 36, ,, 6, ,,   " my "   ,, " mine."
 ,, 37, ,, 3, ,, " thy " & " my " ,, " thine " and " mine."
 ,, 39, ,, 12, ,,   " lay "   ,, " lay'st."
 ,, 51, ,, 12, ,, " those "   ,, " her."
 ,, 53, ,, 3, *from* " Dead " *to* " ashes " should be in inverted commas
 ,, 54, ,, 20, ,,   " or "   ,, " nor."
 ,, 55, ,, 4, ,,   " has "   ,, " hath."
 ,, 59, ,, 10, ,,   " or "   ,, " nor."
 ,, 69, ,, 8, ,,   " that "   ,, " thy," and imagine asterisks between
                                                stanzas 1 and 2.

 ,, 70, ,, 3, ,,   " are,"   " art."
 ,, 71, ,, 2, ,,   " thy "   ,, " thine."
 ,, 84, ,, 2, ,, " Dost thou " ,, " do ye."
 ,, ,, ,, 3, ,, " Art thou " ,, " Are ye."
 ,, ,, ,, 3, ,, " friend "   ,, " friends."
 ,, ,, ,, 4, ,, " Can'st thou " ,, " Can ye."
 ,, ,, ,, 14, ,, " thou hast " ,, " ye have."
 ,, 85, ,, 3, ,,   " thee "   ,, " you."

A. T. W.